WHAT IS YOUR DREAM?

WHAT IS YOUR DREAM?

JOHN KORSZYK

ReadersMagnet, LLC

What Is Your Dream?
Copyright © 2023 by John Korszyk

Published in the United States of America
ISBN   Paperback: 978-1-960629-91-3
ISBN   eBook: 978-1-960629-92-0

All rights reserved. No part of this publication may be reproduced, stored in a retrieval system or transmitted in any way by any means, electronic, mechanical, photocopy, recording or otherwise without the prior permission of the author except as provided by USA copyright law.

The opinions expressed by the author are not necessarily those of ReadersMagnet, LLC.

ReadersMagnet, LLC
10620 Treena Street, Suite 230 | San Diego, California, 92131 USA
1.619. 354. 2643 | www.readersmagnet.com

Book design copyright © 2023 by ReadersMagnet, LLC. All rights reserved.

Cover design by Tifanny Curaza
Interior design by Dorothy Lee

Table of Contents

Foreword 7
Introduction 10

CHAPTER I
Self Discipline 15
CHAPTER II
Dreams Come True 29
CHAPTER III
Paddling Your Canoe Towards Self-Improvement 44
CHAPTER IV
To Be Loved Is The Key To Everything 51
CHAPTER V
Our Deep Need For Acceptance 57
CHAPTER VI
Different Worlds 63
CHAPTER VII
True Friendships 67
CHAPTER VIII
A Successful Dating Relationship 72
CHAPTER IX
You Can't Improvise The Marriage Covenant 82
CHAPTER X
Tests To Confirm Your Vocation 85

Conclusion 90
About The Author 93

FOREWORD

I congratulate Pastor John Korszyk for such a timely and excellent book, What Is Your Dream?, filled with valuable advice for every young person, but also for people in general, who are looking to excel and succeed in this life. I love the main theme of greatness that is within reach for today's youth, which Korszyk shares throughout this book. This transformative material will be used to help and produce a new generation of young people who excel and are victorious throughout Latin America and the entire world in the different career paths where they choose to invest their lives.

All through this book, the author presents fantastic advice filled with wisdom, tried and tested throughout the centuries, that has transformed entire generations to be successful and victorious, and will continue to do so. To quote one: "Choose to use the tools of the Kingdom, and God will support your wise decision of continued self-improvement."

I have known John Korszyk for more than thirty years and have always known him to be someone who seeks and practices the excellence found in Christ Jesus in every area of his life: in his family, in his ministry and service to Christ, in his studies, his personal life, and in all the successes he has achieved in his forty years of ministry. He has always stood out for being an excellent and admirable servant of God.

WHAT IS YOUR DREAM?

I met him in 1988, at the Christian Crusade of Long Beach, California, when he was the Director of Hispanic Ministries. There we ministered together for six years, traveling all over Latin America teaching seminars for young people, pastors, political leaders, college students, national leaders and many other groups. In these ministry trips, I was able to get to know the author very well, and to see his love for Christ and for the wisdom found in the Word of God. I observed how John's heart has alway been about helping the youth to achieve excellence and victory. He would spend his time reading books and writing truths that greatly blessed all those who heard them.

John and I graduated from Fuller Theological Seminary in Pasadena, California, where they taught us to find transformational truths for today's world.

He put these into practice in his own life and became a successful and admirable servant of God, desiring to see families that are healthy and youth that are overflowing with all the blessings that God has for this new generation.

This book is a jewel that must be discovered and read by all young people throughout the whole world. God will use it to bless and transform millions of youth, making them victorious and successful in every dream and project they undertake. Every father, teacher, and youth leader needs to make sure that their youth and children read the wisdom found in this work, which I recommend to those who wish to enjoy the excellence that God has available for everyone.

I congratulate you John, for allowing God and His Holy Spirit to use you to write these lovely and powerful biblical truths, which will be tools from God for the transformation of millions of young people around the world.

Your friend and fellow worker in service to Christ, Dr. Sergio Navarrete Vice-president of the Worldwide Hispanic Brotherhood of the Assemblies of God Superintendent of the Southern Pacific District of the Assemblies of God in the U.S.

INTRODUCTION

A while ago I gave a series of talks at a high school. My goal being that the audience would be able to better themselves in the area of vocation. That is, that the students would be motivated to discover their own potential within and take advantage of the education they were receiving.

This is what every young person needs in order to have the chance to succeed!

In the same way, my desire is that the advice in this book would be applicable to all. That it be easily accessible when facing the future, helpful in achieving one's goals and dreams in the face of challenges, and that the instruction, teaching, and information received be beneficial.

What I share in the following pages comes as a result of students and teachers sharing their experiences of different methods of grading and accountability, that allows for the development of techniques that promote a better use of intelligence when it comes time to study. Many times we hear the saying: "Knowledge is power." But that is not necessarily the case. Those ones who understand this or understand that, in fact, applied knowledge is power! Therefore, it is vital for it to be observed in this context: Knowledge that does not illustrate does not help when it comes to matters that are intellectual.

I want to introduce three basic qualifiers, which I will be building on throughout the entire book: Being excellent, being outstanding, and setting - yourself apart. I will be writing about each of these concepts, which have a special meaning for education. I will put them in context so that it will be clear to you which one of these you need to achieve and apply to your own life.

Having clarity will inspire you to be productive, to work towards your own goals in order to achieve what you desire and fulfill your life purpose. Do you think this is something unreachable in the days we live in? In fact, it is required in order to achieve the very best in life. It is possible.

As King Solomon said: "For everything there is a season, a time for every activity under heaven" (Ecclesiastes 3:1).

A friend who read a portion of this manuscript wrote me the following:

"There are things that have been put in this world to beautify, to serve as background, but which are destined to fade away. They don't have the ability nor the possibility to grow into anything. Man, on the other hand, has been created to grow always and in every way."

Dear reader, this book is written in sections, and in each one of them a light illuminates the possibilities that exist for everyone. I emphasize this, because my concern is and always will be for you to be able to achieve your goals.

I will share what may help you overcome your limitations, what we sometimes call "mediocrity." To a certain degree, I consider that mediocrity unfortunately is and always will be a consequence of not developing a good habit of reading. This is especially true due to the little effort that is put into studying.

In order to interpret the reality of how you see the world, I hope that you can have an open mind. As a teacher, I can tell you that in order to achieve superior levels of comprehension, you must increase the time you spend reading, go further in your study of the material that is being covered, and read a great number of pages. You must also accept the other challenges recommended by an academic schedule so that your achievement will be above the average in class requirements. Making that commitment will cause you to be more determined and will allow you to dream; however, it will not be achieved if you harbor a negative attitude in your view of the world.

How do we get out of that negative attitude? By establishing a proactive mentality, that is, choosing to take notes that are useful and can be applied. This will cause your activity and experience to go up, and of course, you will become more intelligent and feel strong.

In order to become more disciplined, young people who receive this advice gain motivation, learning competency in reinforcing their integrity with determination and consistency in their objectives and goals. The trials and experiences of life are part of the process for continued growth.

Keep your hopes alive, choose to fight; with that attitude everything else will be added to you and you will become a studious young person, full of dreams. You will realize that this is not as complicated as it seems, because you have found knowledge in your regular reading of the book of wisdom, the Word of God, which strengthens you and causes you to progress towards your desired end goal.

In your journey you will see that your own judgement can be subjected to consideration by having an open mind, and by allowing others to contribute with their experiences as they can add details that might enrich your own.

I thank, with all my heart, all the people who have given me their support and assistance in the editing of this text. From the time I began writing - What Is Your Dream? until the point it is was published, the whole process has gone beyond my expectations.

My desire to write this book arose from conversations with many young people who shared their concerns and problems that prevented them from bettering themselves in the academic, spiritual and social settings. I know that what is shared here will bring them to greater success.

It is evident that the only thing keeping educational institutions growing is having students who are diligent and fulfilled. Furthermore, the objective of the text you are reading is to inspire you to put all this into practice and for you to increase your desire to look at a horizon full of hope. Keep your dreams alive because it is the only way to be successful in the midst of adversity.

I hope you will continue to work on bettering yourself and that you would make your time count in the area of academics, in friendship, in dating, and in marriage, like the exceptional young person that you are.

CHAPTER I
SELF DISCIPLINE

"In a brief span of time, your career and your dream change your mentality."

In every matter, the emphasis is on winning the battle with yourself, as that is the only way you will be able to develop a strong and balanced character. Applying self discipline will motivate you to move forward, so that you will continue to imitate the model demonstrated by those who haven't lost the human touch. Be fully committed to the projects you seek to complete.

The Catholic theologian John Newman wrote the following: "Fear not that your life will come to an end, but rather that it shall never have a beginning."

Keeping this in mind, I will introduce some corrective actions, and take definitions and notable examples of dreamers who haven't allowed themselves to become paralyzed "in sleep" but rather "awakened" by their emotions, giving them free reign towards creativity. An important part of the process is creativity, and being certain of where you are going. You will discover this as you go forward, since you alone can decide who enters and who leaves your life.

It is necessary to find out what your personal goals are. Each person needs to know the starting point of their endeavor and in what direction their effort is headed in order to accomplish their life purpose. Once you can picture it, you will move forward from your starting point with greater passion. With the degree you received in hand, you will then be able to begin an exciting journey. Achieving the goals you have set for yourself, knowing that you are performing to your full potential, and with humility to learn from others as well as receiving constructive criticism; this will help you in optimizing what you have learned.

It is a good opportunity to recognize you are encouraging the possibility of motivation and your desire to do a good job. From there you need to think positively that you will indeed improve your grades.

It can be said with certainty that each person is facing a unique opportunity to demonstrate their discipline, efforts, and personal interests. You are headed for success! What a tremendous challenge!

Each person, through their own efforts, can have a positive expectation and achieve good grades for their work.

Every student is required to do a lot of schoolwork; there is an abundance of multifaceted tasks. But now you have an opportunity to be better than the rest, to stand out when creativity awakens in you. It is likely you are someone who

realizes it is necessary to work hard, otherwise, if you have low grades you will end up without advantages.

I trust that God will show you what will help in the preparation and carrying out of your own dreams. We have to make a distinction between what seems to be good as opposed to something that actually ends up being excellent and achieving that excellence in our lives. What

I have observed through the years is that after graduation, students refuse to continue training themselves through the typical challenges of their careers, so that they can live to the full potential of what the Lord has placed in their lives. That is why I want to share my experience with you, which will help you gain perspective through my reality as a person and student. I believe that what is most important, is not making or accumulating money, but rather, that God's presence would be made manifest through each individual, being genuine, real, and authentic.

Some young people may express themselves negatively regarding their careers, because they didn't show any passionate interest in their abilities or in their potential possibilities. They are not fond of challenges. As a result of this lack of vision, they do not change. If they have experienced failure, it doesn't motivate them to work towards success. How are you now? Have you noticed a change in yourself after having taken a class or learning a new subject? Maybe you didn't appreciate your teachers or the content in your required classes? There will always be someone that doesn't value what is being taught at the time, but I must warn you: If you want to avoid academic failure in the future, do not be indifferent. Perhaps your answer today might be: "I believe that transformation will flow naturally and effortlessly in my own life and in my schoolwork, although I know I will make mistakes." I think that is the wrong mindset. Think about it; you won't achieve anything if you live with a dream that is half fulfilled. Much of the path is still before you, and you must choose to travel your own journey. It is valuable to recognize the natural ability a person has as long as it is not ineffective.

The psychologist Abraham Maslow said the following, regarding the law of the instrument: "When all you have is a hammer, every problem looks like a nail." You must pay attention, because you live in fascinating times in regards to learning, and there is a great variety of tools at your disposal. In my role as a motivator, I have had people look into the importance of their way of thinking. To educate themselves in different ways so as to try and understand, choosing the various academic resources that are beneficial to them, deciding which path to take and how to arrive at the goal of excellence. A student can say they "graduated." However, the degrees, titles, and credentials they have received are just the starting point of their growth. Because from that moment, the possibility of reaching what they have been longing for is there. But many don't get there because they harbor confusing and discouraging emotions. Be patient and don't give up if you haven't achieved it yet!

Therefore, from the perspective of education and studies, I encourage students to not waste their time with meaningless, empty, or ambiguous things that do not contribute much.

Time is the most valuable asset you have, and you must not allow yourself the luxury of wasting it. What you need is to be creative, and to look to the Teacher for creativity: To Jesus, through whom all things were made. Precisely, through this Him you can be transformed into a different person, because He loves you unlike anyone else. This conviction allows you to put God as the priority in your life, because of a desire to return that love. Knowing you are valuable; you can face whatever goals you set forth for yourself and be the beneficiary of an excellent conduct. Those who accept Jesus as their Lord know they can count on Christ's victory in every area of their lives.

He has a purpose, and if you are faithful to Him, He will provide you with the resources to develop your character and be able to face life. He places in you the right vision so that you will grow, not only personally but vocationally. He also gives the ability to serve others with love and pure motives, so that your human qualities, in daily life, are at a higher level.

When we read about the life of Jesus in the Gospels, we hear it said: "I have spoken openly to the world" (John 18:20). God continues to speak to us personally today and each one of us can go to Him in any situation and find answers.

When my wife and I are invited to speak at conferences, we seek to share our experiences honestly with the hope that this will encourage the youth to move forward with their dreams of academic achievement. To summarize, if you define your motivations appropriately and you choose to take the path of excellence within God's will, a promising future awaits you.

You will achieve it through three key steps: One: Excellence

Two: Your dreams, directed in God's purposes to be outstanding as a result of being endowed with the ability to be creative.

Three: Set yourself apart and excel, because you know who you are without having to compete to be or appear to be superior to others, but rather, emphasize what is indeed in you.

Of course, we need to make a distinction between what is good and what is bad. Nevertheless, our emphasis has to do with the qualities that define and drive the yearning for true influence. For me, this is true of anyone who excels in their treatment of others.

It also depends on respecting everyone, which is a matter of character. Something established in people who are known for their integrity and the authenticity of their creativity.

This helps fulfill dreams that have to do with grades achieved by "explicitly transmitted education" and well offered by the professors. During every age, there were people who studied, consciously knowing that they had to have initiative, and it helped them to understand that their intellectual capacity, combined with their initiative, improved or increased their chances of success.

A paraphrase of the biblical passage that I mention below will give you guidance as to the plan of action to follow; and if you are a young person with pure motives, it will help you to develop well both in your vocational and your spiritual life.

God's saving grace, you see, appeared for all people. It teaches us that we should turn our backs on ungodliness and the passions of the world, and should live sober, just and devout lives in the present age, while we wait eagerly for the blessed hope and royal appearing of the glory of our great God and savior, Jesus the King. 14 He gave himself for us so that he could ransom us from all lawless actions and purify for himself a people as his very own who would be eager for good works (Titus 2:11-14, NTE).

It is key to understand that it doesn't matter where you were born or what you have. What is important is to understand that you need to live your life in a way that is pleasing to God, not just to you. This is why you must take stock of your life from a young age. On the one hand, choosing what will be constructive in the end, on the other hand, getting ahead of or preventing that which could ruin the plan you have.

For this reason, I suggest that you learn to distinguish, understand, and practice. And I hope I have awakened in you enough of an interest that you will continue reading.

With these concepts in mind, you can make a list that will show you what you need to do in order to achieve excellence in everything you do. Otherwise, you will waste your time on meaningless things without finding new ways of thinking that will lead you to establish the "what" and the "why" of your actions. By applying these tools, you will ultimately become an outstanding individual.

As Christians we are children of the light; holy. I cannot stop emphasizing the importance of moral values in a society that is slipping down into moral decline. As persons of influence wherever we find ourselves, we must be examples. Our lives touch many people. Because of this, everything that relates to friendship, dating, and marriage is of chief importance. Good or bad choices can bring you to resounding success or terrible failure.

This is why you need to stay alert as to what is beneficial, according to the goal you have set for yourself, and choose to carry out your work with the greatest effectiveness possible. There are many factors which contribute to you being a winner. One of these is to face life with a victorious attitude to deal with fear, or fear of failure. Perhaps because you are young, it may be one of your first challenges, but don't get scared. Examine your emotions, thoughts, and actions.

Among the techniques you can use, imagining or reviewing your goals can be useful to see whether they are unrealistic or realistic, and how you perceive yourself, conducting your life in front of others. One's social life is extremely important as a young person, and I have often heard youth say that seeking to feel accepted takes up a lot of their time. Not only do they have to face academic challenges but also the pressure of being rejected by their peers. At other times, it is the demand of the subjects they must study which cause them to feel anxious, and so they come to me for advice.

As a result, relationships play an important role, and if the young person finds himself part of a team, and has strong connections with his classmates, it will be easier for him to deal with the competitiveness that is rife in these environments. What they need is not "an instant dose of courage," but to feel themselves capable of getting on peacefully and being able to take responsibility as their careers progress. This will require that they stay focused and work hard, which is why, just as one must practice before a match, the young person - he or she - must go through training and preparation. Remember, hard work is the secret of a great winner: Play on your team and don't fumble a pass, missing the chance to be in the moment.

I want to emphasize the following: The years of our youth is the period in which we can combine our education with the formation of our character. It is the time when we should be making the type of choices that lead us to become individuals who stand out from the rest. The time when we choose to be different, set apart, upright, determined, and confident in our goals, having exceptional human qualities. The good news is that through my recommendations, and by putting into practice the concepts I develop in this book, you will achieve it!

Remember what we were discussing at the beginning: It is one thing to be excellent another thing to be outstanding and something very different to set your "self-apart" or distinguished in what you do.

If you pay attention to what you set for yourself, you will become that person! You will see the benefits of having clear and well-defined dreams.

There are some keys to recognizing the real choices so that we can take advantage of them. I remember reading a brochure from The U.S. Postal Inspection Service speaking on the precautions one must take to not fall victim to a scam or fraud. The brochure said that we should not trust the following situations. Warnings Signs:

> "Sounds too good to be true.
> Pressures you to act "right away."
> Guarantees success.
> Promises unusually high returns.
> Requires an upfront investment – even for a "free" price.

Buyers want to overpay you for an item and have you send them the difference.
Doesn't have the look of a real business.
Something just doesn't feel right."

PLAY IT SAFE

Never click on a link inside an e-mail to visit a Web site.

Type the address into your browser instead.

It's easy for a business to look legitimate online. If you have any doubts, verify the company with Better Business Bureau.

Only 2% of reported identify theft occurs through the mail. Report online fraud to the Federal Trade Commission atftc.gov/complaint.

Retain your receipts, statements, and packing slips.

Review them for accuracy.

Shred confidential documents instead of simply discarding them in the trash"

Published by Guy J. Cottrell

CHIEF POSTAL INSPECTOR

US Postal Inspection Service ATTN Mail Fraud

We should not be looking for unethical strategies or ways to manipulate in order to get what we want. The effects of deceit and dirty and fraudulent tactics are despicable.

Everything we do, we must do it in love, upholding the fact that God has given us our every talent and ability, and if we achieve success, it will be because He himself put the required excellence in us, and through the circumstances and challenges we may have to face, He might test our obedience. If we put into practice what He has taught us, we will prove ourselves to be faithful. God wants us to grow in our faith and in the assurance of who we are and what we carry, until we become victorious.

Many years ago, King David expressed it in a psalm:

> Do not fret because of those who are evil
> or be envious of those who do wrong;
> for like the grass they will soon wither,
> like green plants they will soon die away.
> Trust in the Lord and do good;
> dwell in the land and enjoy safe pasture.
> Take delight in the Lord,
> and he will give you the desires of your heart.
> Commit your way to the Lord;
> trust in him and he will do this:
> He will make your righteous reward shine like the dawn,
> your vindication like the noonday sun.
> Be still before the Lord
> and wait patiently for him;
> do not fret when people succeed in their ways,
> when they carry out their wicked schemes.
> Refrain from anger and turn from wrath;
> do not fret—it leads only to evil.
> —Psalm 37:1-8 NIV.

WHAT IS YOUR DREAM?

For this reason, in regard to who God is, we see that at times He remains silent during a trial, testing us to see if He remains our priority and if we trust Him completely.

Let me be very clear in regards to the three steps mentioned before for excellence:

Step one: Because you have in your being innate abilities from your Creator, you must grow in these yourself. Do you remember the example of Joseph? The son of Jacob (Israel) accurately interpreted the dreams of the baker and cupbearer of the royal court, and in surprise, the Egyptian Pharaoh exclaimed: "Can we find anyone like this man, one in whom is the Spirit of God" (Genesis 41:38)

The level of excellence in which Joseph proceeded and his trust and faithfulness to God caused him to come and live in the palace and govern all of Egypt. He was given the crown and scepter from the most supreme authority and he became the highest-ranking political leader in the Egyptian empire, second only to Pharaoh himself.

Step two: Allow God's dreams to be made manifest in you, just as we see in Joseph's life. Because your desires include aspects that reveal themselves as possibilities and are deep inside of you, try to identify them and do not stop them just because your current situation might not be ideal. Allow your aspirations to take flight. Don't lose sight of the fact that the aim is for each person to become outstanding, and for this you do not need to limit yourself in the things you want to achieve.

And step three: Encourage yourself, work hard to define the goals you want to achieve in order to set yourself apart and be recognized for your work. For this, you will have to think, read and write more. Don't settle until the good becomes something better, and the best becomes excellent.

This requires us to be creative and to keep our eyes looking forward, determined to live life in a way that we stand out from that which is average. It is what allows dreams to become reality. For this, you will have to keep an open mind in order to appreciate your own abilities and talents.

So, choose to be better every day, and later you will be able to share with others how you got there, using your own life as a benchmark.

As you go through adolescence, you overcome your shyness and become more open to the possibility of responsibly choosing your path in life and enjoying achievements in regard to how you express yourself, as well as the attitudes that make you feel most comfortable. What you desire for yourself will begin to sprout in your mind and in your heart, then you will want to share it and spread your perfume, and wherever you go, your personality will be revealed. You can put your faith in the fact that, in Jesus, and by depending on Him, you will achieve everything you have set for yourself.

Nurturing an intimate relationship with Jesus will make you an extraordinary person. What all of us want in our lives is to see positive results, and as we look back through the years, we want to be able to prove that we lived a life full of meaningful accomplishments.

This way of living has spiritual significance and it must be understood through the Holy Scriptures, that all good things come from above, from our God.

May God encourage you with the words He spoke in the Old Testament through Jeremiah 29:11:

"For I know the plans I have for you," declares the Lord, "plans to prosper you and not to harm you, plans to give you hope and a future."

This is how God is: He seeks after us and is near to teach us so truths that are excellent, outstanding, and set apart.

Your "graduation day" will be an unforgettable moment you should truly enjoy, knowing that it is confirming in you those qualities which will allow you to fulfill your role or function for which you have prepared. These are talents which have been given to you and seem natural to you, and yet they have been placed there by the One who created you. Do not, however, be unappreciative in any way of those who have contributed to your development and have provided you with the opportunity to grow. Both you and your family deserve to have a good outcome!

God is the only path to true success; it is amazing to walk with Him. Consequently, you must set aside "foolish things," those things that distract and prevent you from reaching your desired goal.

In the following chapters, I will provide you with some ideas on how to go about achieving excellence, standing apart, and being outstanding in every area of your life.

CHAPTER II
DREAMS COME TRUE

When a person is young, he or she has a lot of dreams. The good news is that many of them can come true. If we walk with Jesus, He leads us to an abundant life because He has a promising future for every person, and you can be transformed and go higher and higher, according to the amount of maturity you develop.

Unfortunately, it grieves me to say that many young people live their lives without taking God into account. But those who do are aware that God has created them and knows what they can accomplish. And if you don't completely understand what He expects from you, you can turn to the Bible, which is a type of manual that allows you to find direction to guide you and challenge you to go forward through hard work and dedication. You will have at your disposal spiritual power, wisdom, advice and references, answers to your existential questions and a guide to go far in your quest to achieve excellence.

Let us look at an example in the Book of Proverbs: "Listen, my sons, to a father's instruction; pay attention and gain understanding. The beginning of wisdom is this: Get wisdom. Though it cost all you have, get understanding." Young people find that the Book of Ecclesiastes talks about things that are senseless, meaningless and vain; that is, things that are unimportant (we must avoid the practice of foolishness and profanity). The word "meaningless" appears about 35 times in the Book of Ecclesiastes:

"The neglect of those who despise wisdom and consistent teaching, do not take God into account, because wisdom is respecting and acknowledging God and his teachings." (Excerpt from Proverbs, chapters 1 and 4).

You were created to be attuned to the directions of the Creator:

"The fear of the Lord is the beginning of knowledge, but fools despise wisdom and instruction" (Proverbs 1:).

God wants you to:

"Get wisdom, get understanding" (Proverbs 4:5).

"Tell me who you love, and I will tell you who you are," declares the Creole Proverb. But I also say: "Biblical truths are the principles by which God rules our lives." Because of all cultural heritage, with its particularity and also the respect that we owe our forefathers, originates primarily in the Word of God. There are principles with defined foundations that we call "universal." For example, the institution of marriage is for many, accepted as a civil contract. For Christians it is a deep bond based on a marriage covenant, in which each person, by declaring their vows, commits to love, care, and be faithful to the other. This brings a mutual blessing as well as mutual benefits to both parties. But, because of the heterogeneity (diversity) of cultures that exist around the world, we see that some values of our cultural heritage are on the path to extinction, since their paths are not those of our forefathers, fathers and grandfathers.

People's plans and destinies are varied; nothing is boring or bland. Life is active, constant; our thoughts, attitudes, and actions are being transformed, as we allow God's Word to renew us and lead us away from fear. You can face small frustrations and find courage to not give up or get stuck halfway through your journey to fulfilling your dreams.

We know that nobody wants that. Therefore, do not get discouraged if you feel that you have not achieved much just yet. Keep going forward, determined to gain success, and recognize that in the midst of difficulties and moments of weakness, many have been able to excel and stand out.

The Kingdom of God has its own resources and God will support you if you have decided to better yourself. God's very power is within your reach and available in order to serve Him with passion and with the resources you have.

If you allow the Word of God to transform you, you won't settle for mediocrity, which is an evil that afflicts many in their way of thinking, feeling, and living. They don't discern what is right in their inner being and as a result, they wander aimlessly in empty spiritual paths. But if you have decided to follow the path of excellence, your values will be different; to be humble and consider others just as valuable as yourself.

Each person should hold onto a higher purpose in life without despising what they have, but neither should they become proud. Rather, they should be level-headed, having a healthy sense of who they are. Identity matters.

What Is Your Dream?

It may happen that as a result of your lack of experience, you become afraid of facing challenges, believing beforehand that you will fail. It's not easy for some of us to believe that we can maintain a high level of performance.

What I would like to tell you is that the best way to avoid frustration is to equip yourself properly, to be willing to study and learn. Be organized and try to be useful, always willing to obey God and your teachers. God has provided you with physical, intellectual, moral, and spiritual skills. You are always qualified to help others.

Remember Joseph, who correctly interpreted Pharaoh's dreams. He gathered his courage and the first battle he won was the battle against himself, when he rid himself of all the timidity in his heart in order to help others. You have personal skills which can be put in the service of others, among these, your ability to love. We are always challenged to serve and not live only for our own enjoyment. Serving our neighbor gives us a sense of fulfillment and increases our self- esteem. We feel useful and satisfied; even more so if people recognize our unconditional support and realize our sincerity. These qualities arise because we are obedient to Jesus and are willing to offer ourselves, surrendering our selfishness, our desire to have our way, or our competitiveness.

God rewards our obedience, allowing us to reach that which pleases and reflects in us His qualities. It is an effective ctivation of the Kingdom's values in our humanness, and it becomes the natural process of those who believe in God. As you go forward, you have to think about the steps you will take. Planning matters.

This is what David did in his remarkable victory against the giant Goliath.

"You come against me with sword and spear and javelin, but I come against you in the name of the Lord Almighty, the God of the armies of Israel" (1 Samuel 17:45).

What really matters in the life of the human being is to make good use of "today." By making wise and sound decisions about your life, it will allow you to prosper in all the paths you take, and your self-confidence will grow.

Your studies, your work, your contributions to society, those you help with household chores, or even the help you give your college classmates places a firm and efficient foundation upon your character. You know yourself better and your innate potential increases. In contrast, some go to university full of fantasies or mere illusions, with the typical adolescent immaturity, and they don't choose to have a vision or idea of what they want to be in the future. Consequently, they don't take time or pay attention to those things that are required in order to achieve and implement changes. It remains to be seen then, if they understand how life is so fleeting, sensual pleasure so temporal, and bliss so brief in contrast to the value of building a balanced life with eternal principles. Balance matters.

Many young people in Latin America have thanked us for having motivated them to be victorious in life. A young woman wrote us the following: "Good day, beloved pastor. God bless you! When you were in Buenos Aires, Argentina, you preached about fear; I was 14 years old. You spoke about people who have fears. At that time, I was feeling very afraid, since I was a teenager with my whole life ahead of me. Your message touched me and completely changed me.

You said that the LOVE of God casts away fear, and you preached on that theme and I was touched because I thought: If God's love casts away fear, I must cover myself and live in God's love. If the love of God is in me, there shouldn't be any fear. My life was changed from that day forward. I am so grateful to you for being an instrument in God's hand. Blessings!"

Those who trust in the infinite love of our Heavenly Father do better. In those moments in their walk when they are faced with challenges that look like insurmountable walls they don't think they'll be able to scale, they will experience the love of the Father, giving them the strength to excel and deal with the problem they have in front of them. For this reason, you need to lay strong foundations in order to build up your life with goals, hopes, and meaningful dreams.

I would like for each young person to glimpse their dreams as if they were flashes of greatness, and so be able to become a champion. In every student, from the beginning of their studies in elementary school until university, a seed begins to sprout that could set the student apart from the rest. This is why it is important for you to have a clear idea of what you want as you go forward.

"Hardships often prepare ordinary people for an extraordinary destiny." —C.S. Lewis.

You have to focus and concentrate on what is good! That must be your daily goal. And trust that God will show you what is best for your life!

Paul, the author and apostle of the early church, recommended to his readers a better way. He told them: "And yet I will show you the most excellent way" (1 Corinthians 12:31). Paul spoke to them of something we can all aspire to: The extraordinary. God knows you, and He can use what he put in you to help you picture what He has in mind. As a result, you can look to the future with hope. Our life is a process and it begins right here today; it is what will finally help you reach the future you yearn for. Don't stop once you've thought about what you want; perhaps your goal is to graduate Summa Cum Laude, i.e. with the highest honors. It is a noble aspiration to want to be a young man or woman who is honorable, outsanding, and an example by finding the way in which your dreams allow you to be the sail that guides your destiny in the sea of possibilities.

On the other hand, many consider the genuine aspiration of reaching greater achievements as something lacking value, since they have no desire but to "live in the moment." They don't even think about how to achieve personal growth. In contrast, those who are victorious, like the athlete who runs in a marathon, cannot spend their time with distractions or big meals; that would be a waste. Idle time that would hurt their training. Unfortunately, this is what happens when people don't act in a balanced manner or with the correct perspective.

Business, marketing, and entertainment promoters attempt to manipulate children and young people's attention and motivation towards interests that are empty but financially profitable. They could care less that they waste their time on video games and tv. It's obvious that those young people who were smitten with that sell only want what is easy, fast, and comfortable, instead of all the effort that is required to complete a university degree in order to get a good job; something that they generally see as cold and competitive.

In order to have enough light to discern the meaning of what I am saying, it is necessary for you to realize that we are novices in terms of what society puts in front of us, but we must be alert to understand which things add value and which are damaging. You cannot only think about gratifying your senses in the moment.

One of the issues that can bring terrible confusion at an age where the emphasis should be on studies, is the subject of using sexuality as entertainment and making a show of it without accountability. As part of their college life, many students have made a habit of going to parties, and many of these include drugs and alcohol, which are ruining lives full of promise and causing quite a bit of family breakdown.

Having fun and celebrating is not wrong. College students need to have breaks from their intensive schedule of studies (intellectual fatigue) as a result of their effort to get good grades, but what is being promoted today is turning healthy fun into an extreme experience of sexual excess. Distractions are important in order to relax and they contribute towards learning, but fun and games need to run through natural outflows and not through physical or emotional excesses.

Our current culture promotes what is frivolous, superficial, and temporal, and doesn't emphasize those things that truly satisfy and are permanent. Banal entertainment gives way to casual sexual interactions resulting in an emotional disconnect and the emptiness produced by having relations that are not based on love. The sexual act should be the deepest expression of love between two individuals. Instead, it has been corrupted in such a way that casual sexual encounters have become the norm, which in turn brings emotional weariness and deceitful promises of faithfulness that only serve to meet sensual pleasures.

Young people should encourage moments of camaraderie, but not lose sight of the future that lies before them and stay focused on the season of preparation. Remember that "success happens when your dreams are bigger than your excuses." Being aware of these things will give you confidence to reach your goals; never doubt that you are accepted and chosen for a life of excellence.

God has plans for the dreamers "Dreams come true in the years of youth, divine treasure." When you choose to follow your path by allowing the Lord to guide you, He will take you from one level of faith to the next and you will have the power to reach your dreams, as you begin to understand them more clearly. Jesus reveals to you the Father and the plans He has for you. He is "the way" you walk in your spiritual path. If you have God, you have everything, and His abundant resources are available to you. It is a pity that some don't keep this in mind. This is why God invites you to dream.

"A youth that doesn't feed on his dreams, quickly grows old" - William Shakespeare.

This is why walking with God is so important. It is an essential part of success, as Ignatius of Loyola stated:

"Take, Lord, and receive all my liberty, my memory, my understanding, and my entire will, all I have and call my own. You have given all to me. To you, Lord, I return it. Everything is yours; do with it what you will. Give me only your love and your grace, that is enough for me."

Having a personal relationship with Jesus will cause you to achieve extraordinary results. Each and every one of us certainly wants that. But don't ask Jesus to guide your steps if you are not willing to move your feet. This way of life is about the everyday and it must be supported by the Word of God, which will transform you; renew your mind and heart to grasp what God desires and has prepared for you.

In the book of the prophet Jeremiah, in chapter 29 verse 11, God encourages us to go forward with these words:

"For I know the plans I have for you," declares the Lord, "plans to prosper you and not to harm you, plans to give you hope and a future."

Relating these concepts to learning, I see that a lot of people are presented with extraordinary opportunities to prove their abilities, and the testing method that is disliked by many is necessary for assessing their level. It is a challenge to reach better academic achievements. It is the way to connect the dreams regarding the advancement of one's career and the real goals that must be set in order to achieve them. The content must reach the deepest part of the mind, so that the brain will grasp the knowledge being offered and so acquire wisdom. As a result of the potential God has gifted you with, you can live according to the wisdom that He gives; and certainly you will know how to wisely apply what you have learned! To think otherwise, is to deny the challenge that each person has the opportunity to go forward until they become better, willing to be excellent, outstanding, and set themselves apart.

If you'd like, you can pray like this:

"Lord Jesus, you broadened my hidden potential; I already see the results. You took me out of a tight place and increased my space, you caused me to prosper, you surrounded me with your favor, even though this is a regular day, yet I see my dreams being fulfilled.

I will not stay the same. Everything will change, until my dreams of excellence and of continuous advancement materialize. I will continue to wait upon You, my God. I know you are pleased with my prayer."

And since we spoke in this chapter about dreams, I would like to continue sharing with you some ideas from God's heart regarding some other areas of interest to you and for which you will surely also have expectations.

Business, marketing, and entertainment promoters attempt to manipulate children and young people's attention and motivation towards interests that are empty but financially profitable. They could care less that they waste their time on video games and tv. It's obvious that those young people who were smitten with that sell only want what is easy, fast, and comfortable, instead of all the effort that is required to complete a university degree in order to get a good job; something that they generally see as cold and competitive.

In order to have enough light to discern the meaning of what I am saying, it is necessary for you to realize that we are novices in terms of what society puts in front of us, but we must be alert to understand which things add value and which are damaging. You cannot only think about gratifying your senses in the moment.

One of the issues that can bring terrible confusion at an age where the emphasis should be on studies, is the subject of using sexuality as entertainment and making a show of it without accountability. As part of their college life, many students have made a habit of going to parties, and many of these include drugs and alcohol, which are ruining lives full of promise and causing quite a bit of family breakdown.

Having fun and celebrating is not wrong. College students need to have breaks from their intensive schedule of studies (intellectual fatigue) as a result of their effort to get good grades, but what is being promoted today is turning healthy fun into an extreme experience of sexual excess. Distractions are important in order to relax and they contribute towards learning, but fun and games need to run through natural outflows and not through physical or emotional excesses.

Our current culture promotes what is frivolous, superficial, and temporal, and doesn't emphasize those things that truly satisfy and are permanent. Banal entertainment gives way to casual sexual interactions resulting in an emotional disconnect and the emptiness produced by having relations that are not based on love. The sexual act should be the deepest expression of love between two individuals. Instead, it has been corrupted in such a way that casual sexual encounters have become the norm, which in turn brings emotional weariness and deceitful promises of faithfulness that only serve to meet sensual pleasures.

Young people should encourage moments of camaraderie, but not lose sight of the future that lies before them and stay focused on the season of preparation. Remember that "success happens when your dreams are bigger than your excuses." Being aware of these things will give you confidence to reach your goals; never doubt that you are accepted and chosen for a life of excellence.

God has plans for the dreamers "Dreams come true in the years of youth, divine treasure." When you choose to follow your path by allowing the Lord to guide you, He will take you from one level of faith to the next and you will have the power to reach your dreams, as you begin to understand them more clearly. Jesus reveals to you the Father and the plans He has for you. He is "the way" you walk in your spiritual path. If you have God, you have everything, and His abundant resources are available to you. It is a pity that some don't keep this in mind. This is why God invites you to dream.

"A youth that doesn't feed on his dreams, quickly grows old" - William Shakespeare.

This is why walking with God is so important. It is an essential part of success, as Ignatius of Loyola stated: "Take, Lord, and receive all my liberty, my memory, my understanding, and my entire will, all I have and call my own. You have given all to me. To you, Lord, I return it. Everything is yours; do with it what you will. Give me only your love and your grace, that is enough for me."

Having a personal relationship with Jesus will cause you to achieve extraordinary results. Each and every one of us certainly wants that. But don't ask Jesus to guide your steps if you are not willing to move your feet. This way of life is about the everyday and it must be supported by the Word of God, which will transform you; renew your mind and heart to grasp what God desires and has prepared for you.

In the book of the prophet Jeremiah, in chapter 29 verse 11, God encourages us to go forward with these words: "For I know the plans I have for you," declares the Lord, "plans to prosper you and not to harm you, plans to give you hope and a future."

Relating these concepts to learning, I see that a lot of people are presented with extraordinary opportunities to prove their abilities, and the testing method that is disliked by many is necessary for assessing their level. It is a challenge to reach better academic achievements. It is the way to connect the dreams regarding the advancement of one's career and the real goals that must be set in order to achieve them. The content must reach the deepest part of the mind, so that the brain will grasp the knowledge being offered and so acquire wisdom. As a result of the potential God has gifted you with, you can live according to the wisdom that He gives; and certainly you will know how to wisely apply what you have learned! To think otherwise, is to deny the challenge that each person has the opportunity to go forward until they become better, willing to be excellent, outstanding, and set themselves apart.

If you'd like, you can pray like this:

"Lord Jesus, you broadened my hidden potential; I already see the results. You took me out of a tight place and increased my space, you caused me to prosper, you surrounded me with your favor, even though this is a regular day, yet I see my dreams being fulfilled.

I will not stay the same. Everything will change, until my dreams of excellence and of continuous advancement materialize. I will continue to wait upon You, my God. I know you are pleased with my prayer."

And since we spoke in this chapter about dreams, I would like to continue sharing with you some ideas from God's heart regarding some other areas of interest to you and for which you will surely also have expectations.

CHAPTER III

PADDLING YOUR CANOE TOWARDS SELF-IMPROVEMENT

In the rapids of your life…

As you move forward at the youthful pace of your age, education, friendships, and feelings, we arrive at points when we must make big decisions about different matters, some of which are unexpected. These matters can require swift decisions, turning in one direction and then another, as if you were surfing in the waves of the ocean. At times you will feel as if you are navigating river rapids, physically and mentally, in a light canoe with only one paddle, facing the threat of a great waterfall unless you give it a strong and precise stroke, just in time to avoid crashing against the rocks.

But you have to remember that God is the one who can guide you in the right course of your own river. You need to value the vital quality of growing in the will and purpose of God. In a world where darkness prevails, it is of utmost importance that God's presence be made manifest in you.

Jesus conquered freedom for us, but the principle that should guide us is the advice given by the Apostle Paul in 1 Corinthians 6:12: "I have the right to do anything…but not everything is beneficial."

As a result, you must establish the way of life you desire, keeping in mind what the divine goals are: To be excellent, outstanding, and set apart. You are to live in the midst of your generation being an influence upon your friends, encouraging them towards good works through your own example and not the other way around.

Let us aim for the true meaning of the life of a winner, one who stands out for being courageous, decisive, taking advantage of opportunities, confident of his or her potential, and fulfilling the role of being an influencer in everything. The fact is that the light shines brightest in the darkness. When we are united with Jesus, and since He lives in us, we are children of the light and our light will shine in Your commitment to Christ is also a commitment to His Kingdom. You must be like a trained soldier, willing to fight the battles, to obey orders, and to be faithful. You must make a commitment to the dream God put inside of you and press forward to achieve it with passion.

In the same way, you can trust that He will guide you when you have to make important decisions regarding your career or your love life. God will give you peace and will steady your emotions so that you are able to seek His will at all times. His direction will sustain and encourage you so that what you dream will become reality.

I am aware of how difficult this time is and how full of changes this period in life can be, and that can make you feel unsure. But C.S. Lewis said on a particular occasion: "Hardships often prepare ordinary people for an extraordinary destiny." Therefore, yours will be a journey where you will achieve your dreams one step at a time, and where the light of God's divine Word will illuminate your path. One day you will declare: "It wasn't easy, but I did it." Don't settle until the good becomes better and the better becomes excellent.

It is difficult to produce the necessary changes under certain conditions, resulting in an inability to react which I call: learned helplessness. This is displayed when too much time is spent copying "s yles or tastes" seen in TV shows or movies, trends and preferences that are assumed as their own but which are not really a good reflection of their personalities. Because, in a sense, it is easier and more comfortable to copy someone else rather than make the effort to embody a unique and enterprising personality.

When we fall into this sort of thing, violence, weaknesses, coasting through life and expecting others to do the hard work, all these take shape in the young mind, which is easily influenced and is distracted from its goals. I don't want this to sound like a rebuke, but rather a way to move forward and be cautious. It is to encourage you to have sound judgment and be intentional in everything you do. May your strength be that of a great conqueror!

This is emphasized to encourage young people to see reality before it takes place. It is to encourage them to have good judgment and specific intentions.

If you maintain a spirit of initiative, and you challenge yourself in your personal life, you will begin to develop a taste for what is excellent, you will feel as if you have been chosen for this transformative process. Little by little you will remove yourself from your parents' protection, finding your own way to relate and interact with your peers. The experiences you will begin to have, based on your faith in the Scriptures will allow you to discern between good and bad, between what is true and what is false. This will allow you to choose those things that will help you focus on those interests that cause you to better yourself, in order to make necessary changes and turn away from negative and despairing attitudes that can end up obscuring your understanding.

From the beginning, I have told you that excellence comes from an active choice, no matter your social condition.

By prioritizing what is spiritual first, you have to commit yourself completely and make that your strength. Always keep an analytical mind regarding the here and now as you propel yourself towards the future.

Therefore I believe that excellence is perfected in the small choices and details that end up being significant in the end. Don't keep going around in circles with outside influences; you need to stand out, set yourself apart from the crowd. Don't give up on reaching the shore, of bringing your boat to your desired destination. By continuing to paddle with your oar, you will become a different person!

In order to overcome the rapids of life with your canoe, you will first have to trust in God's guidance. He will be your compass. You must continually seek Him, so that He will bring you to a good destination. Some people may look down on your youth, and yet this is truly a time in life when we feel we can take the world by storm. It is not for nothing that we often hear the phrase: "Youth, divine treasure." But for those going through that period, it can be an overwhelming time.

In the course of the river that is your life, there are several waterfalls you will have to navigate:

Insecurity. In each and every phase of development, we must deal with insecurities and fears as they relate to different situations and contexts. The stark reality is that during adolescence, these feelings can overwhelm us and affect good performance, especially regarding one's studies.

In order to be able to endure these moments, it's good to have the support of your parents, if you have the blessing of getting along well with them, or a mentor at school or a spiritual advisor. The rule is to not remain silent or alone, and to have the courage to share what is going on in your life. Many fears are created because of a lack of good nutrition or needed rest. With time, you will realize that many of the things we fear and problems that seem to be insurmountable will never actually take place. For this reason, it is advisable to have someone that can help you put your problems in perspective. That is a battle within yourself and we could have a long discussion regarding your sphere of influence (parents, siblings and relatives) with whom you grew up and whether they were able to provide you with a calm, safe environment. If that was not the case, you may often feel anxious, preventing you from forming stable relationships. Do you have a hard time developing a good circle of friends and schoolmates? They will help you to overcome your insecurities, and to be brave enough to ask for what you need, to feel confident and secure even when you feel disappointed. Your self-respect transcends your inability to overcome your frustrations, when you feel stuck, disappointed or go through the most heartbreaking of experiences. You can find a safe refuge when you put your faith in the living God, your Heavenly Father, who loves you so much more than you could ever possibly love Him. Vulnerability matters.

Fear of embarrassment. This feeling is very common in this phase of development. Because of your own insecurity, you will often feel inadequate, out of place, and afraid of looking bad to your friends and classmates. This is because we have such a strong need to feel accepted within our group and to be liked by others. Many young people are introverted, shy, timid or self-conscious, and this is often not because they don't want or don't need to share their ideas or opinions, but because they are afraid to say something that will make them look foolish, consequently, they prefer to keep quiet. As you are able, try to be brave, positive, well-informed, and participate more in meaningful conversations. You must take risks, but your approach to conversation must be wise and seasoned with good manners. You have a lot to offer, and don't be disappointed if at times, things don't turn out like you expected. As I have said, every human being has great value and much to offer to the world.

SHY or bashful: Shyness, it is a feeling of insecurity or shame (about yourself in front of others). When a person is shy or timed they think they will never do anything well, which often causes them to feel anxiety over what others think of them. This feeling can cause physical signs such as sweating, clammy or cold hands, or rapid heartbeats. This can hinder or prevent you from performing well, especially when taking exams or having to give a presentation. To overcome this, you must take a step of faith, and if you realize you cannot, it is ok to seek help, to practice with someone with whom you feel comfortable or to talk about it with a mentor or counselor. When a person begins to take small steps and dares to step outside of themselves, little by little they can gain self-confidence and begin to relax.

Trials and experiences come along, and they are like negotiating rapids with all their twists and turns and variable speed. They are cons antly challenging you to always work hard, gain expertise, and to reach beyond your own abilities. They give you a marker to see how far you've come. But there will be times during these experiences, where you will be tempted, and you may not be ready to deal with this. It is very important during these times to take a moment to examine your conscience and ask yourself if what is being presented is what you desire deep down for your life and how you want to live it.

In this way, you will not only be able to negotiate the boulders in the raging river of life with your canoe, but you will also take flight. Like the eagle you will gain altitude and you will adjust your flying to your own pace. The Holy Spirit will carry you to unimaginable heights, towards the sacred. Today, the cloud represents the place in the heavens where you can store that which is of greater value, what matters to you, what you do not want to lose. There, is where you guard your heart and every achievement. Treasure it like an experience that enriches and brings depth to your life.

CHAPTER IV

TO BE LOVED IS THE KEY TO EVERYTHING

As human beings we were created with basic needs that must be met. One of them is to love and be loved. The first person who seeks our unconditional love is the Lord, and in our hearts, this space should not be filled by anyone else. Even though His command is that we love Him with all our hearts, with all our minds and with all our strength, He also asks that we love our neighbor as ourselves.

No matter how old you are, you need to overcome certain doubts regarding your future, and it isn't always easy to know which path to take. Tomorrow may look confusing and like many pieces of a puzzle spread out. Who should you turn to? In those times the role of a school mentor, an adult you look up to, or a family counselor can be of great help. Typically, this is someone who is more experienced than you are who has been on the journey longer and in the case of those who work with youth, they can be a positive influence when you need encouragement or motivation to seek a career which will best fit with your own talents.

Keep the flame of your passion alive, as well as your mental acuity; be efficient with your time because time that is past, flies, and you can never get it back.

What Is Your Dream?

You live in a time that is completely different to that of your parents. It isn't easy to grasp new cultures and trends, advancements in every sense, what you identify with and what can be misunderstood.

Don't lose sight that you have chosen to be excellent, and if at any time you feel that you are lacking wisdom to know which path to take, remember what the Holy Spirit says through the Apostle James: "If any of you lacks wisdom, you should ask God, who gives generously to all without finding fault, and it will be given to you" (James 1:5).

As the young person that you are, you have to deal with moments of dissatisfaction and not being happy with yourself; nevertheless, that doesn't mean you need to act like others say you should in order to gain their acceptance. Having this in mind, you can develop healthy and warm relationships with your peers that include also helping and serving them. There is a high level of interest in relationships during this period, and that interest will continue throughout your life. We were created to have connection with others; to share life's joys and moments of sadness. It is likely that you will find various strengths in other people, but you will also see their weaknesses helping you understand that no one is perfect and that you must cover other people's faults with love.

It is during this period that your identity will be defined, being close to other people but without the added pressure of physical attraction; the relationships you will develop can be relaxed, deep, fun, and very interesting.

The period of adolescence is about growth; as the meaning of the root word in Latin describes it: "becoming mature and growing up." It is not a bad idea during this time to choose to make it a period of developing and an opportunity to cultivate genuine friendships, without romantic involvement, although you will be attracted to some individuals of the opposite sex or maybe feel more connected to them. As people, we have a need for deep connection, companionship, and being valued.

For this you should also turn to God and ask Him to help you meet people who will be a blessing, who will help you grow and want to be better, not the opposite. So often we are tempted to believe that some ne who is popular, handsome, or even "sexy", should be envied. But you need to understand that people with those perceived characteristics seek to always look good and be noticed, and at times they can be overly superficial. You must be prudent; remind yourself that often, what is important is not necessarily what is visible. During this time, you are amused by what is considered "cool", but now is when lasting and important friendships are born. Nevertheless, some are circumstantial connections, such as being in the same class or practicing the same sport.

During this process of the development of your social life, a natural separation will occur from your dependence on your parents. This is normal, because you are no longer a child and you need to stand on your own. More and more, you will want to interpret events and life experiences to reflect your own interests, convictions, and values.

But perhaps you might feel that it is easier to talk about these subjects with people your own age, discussing it as equals. It is good for you to remember, however, that if you feel unsure about some subject, your parents and teachers can be your mentors and help to clarify any questions you may have. It is a good habit to learn to listen to the opinions of others, allowing you to consider other points of view and understand that not everyone feels the same. Since young people are in the phase of trying to find their own values and convictions, it is likely that they might have a default attitude of being contrary to the thinking of adults and not being able, or choosing not to understand their reasoning. You will surely seek the company of your friends, someone to laugh with and feel accepted, who is honest with you, and makes you feel comfortable. As a Scottish proverb says: "A smile costs less than electricity and it gives more light." Try it and you will see that when you smile, happiness will follow, and if you get in the habit of smiling, difficult circumstances will be easier to bear. Besides, smiles are contagious and create a warm environment around you. Be kind and respectful to others and share a genuine and pleasant smile without feeling the need to fake it.

Friendship is an attitude of being willing to give and receive. It is crucial for these deep feelings to be rooted in your heart! It is the way in which your way of thinking and your doing will interact, and that is essential for developing a good friendship; an honest exchange between your resources and those of the other person.

Be careful with yourself, with your attitudes and your thoughts. Don't seek to always please yourself or even to feel sorry for yourself. Either extreme is harmful to you. It is necessary for your self-esteem to be healthy and for you to be free every day, especially from fear.

I've heard it said: "Fear is a wall that separates who you are from what you could become."

If you need to feel certain regarding who loves you and who doesn't, remember that God's love is perfect. He loved you before you were created. You were in His mind and heart. Only the Lord can fill your inner emptiness because you were created to be loved by Him and to love Him. Only when you can receive His love and realize that He loves you despite all of your flaws, then can you then begin to love yourself. It is only then that you will begin to love someone else. By receiving God's love in your heart, you can then love others.

The first thing the Lord asks of you is to love Him with all your being, heart, and strength so that He can be number one in your life. You need to experience His love and be secure that because He loves you, He wants the best for you and will give you the necessary wisdom along the way to achieve your goals and walk in your destiny. With God's love in your heart, it will not be difficult to love, and others will also return that love!

You can have the certainty that when Jesus is your Lord you can be propelled into your destiny. The truth that makes you free is knowing and living the truth of who He is, for whom He gave His life, and for whom He rose again. Jesus said: "then you will know the truth, and the truth will set you free" (John 8:32). The Lord offers you the right perspective for your personal and vocational growth so that you can serve others with love and pure motives. Now, if you know someone who tells you it is hard to choose what is right and you see them spending a lot of time on trivial and conflictive matters, don't trust them. Seek wisdom and follow it. Figure out what subjects or disciplines you enjoy and which fit well with your temperament. Try them out and practice them, whether they relate to a certain sport, or music, or another art form.

In order to achieve success, you mus think about your potential and what causes you to stand out from the rest, this will cause your dreams to become reality.

If you set a course and decide to follow it, you will be a hard-working student and will receive many pleasant compliments. It will be an honor to have you at any university!

Remember: "Only when a truth begins to be lived does it have the power to change the human being" (R.R. May).

CHAPTER V
OUR DEEP NEED FOR ACCEPTANCE

To be accepted is one of the basic needs of every human being. Having been created by God and in order to have a relationship with Him, our affective system is sensitive to the look of approval or disapproval. We all want to feel like we belong to a community. As a young person, it's likely you believe: "If I accept others just as they are, they will also accept me." But in some way we all have the feeling that we aren't good enough, and it is normal to want others to assure us that we are wrong. However, having an inferiority complex can be overcome little by little if you understand first of all, that the Lord made you, He is your Father, and He loves you just the way you are! The necessary security to overcome an inferiority complex is found by fulfilling the primary need: "To feel loved and to love yourself." You would like others to accept you and not feel less than, however, for that you must make peace with God. Once you accept His love, only then will you be capable of looking to others with care and accept them as they are. Respect, in this case, means understanding that others also have rights that we can violate. And at times, you may not agree with how some people are, but your attitude must be one of patience and not exasperation.

Today we live in a society which promotes selfishness and a life that is focused solely on one's interests.

You probably often butt heads with attitudes that are completely contrary to those that the Bible promotes regarding relationships.

I would like to ask you then: In what social circle do you find examples to follow? During adolescence, a lot of time is spent with family, but even more time is spent with friends, which is normal because of the natural longing one feels to make friends. We grow closer to them, and can also copy many of their examples and behaviors.

As a rule, young people don't think much about developing self-esteem or nurturing a healthy love for themselves. Nor do they consider good habits that will cause them to be better every day. Making friends takes up their attention and is what matters. Being accepted by the group can cause him or her to be tempted and be unfaithful to his or her Christian convictions. It is sad to see that in schools, young people make such a great effort to fit in, to be part of the crowd or a certain group. They can't bear to feel excluded. They don't value their uniqueness, their quirkiness, the fact that they are one-of-a-kind. They don't want to feel unpopular. For this reason, they prefer to copy behaviors that may not be their own, that they don't like, actions that could bother their conscience and things they wouldn't even do in private because of the pressure to be accepted by the group. Keeping this in mind, we can see that some teenagers become involved in physical relationships because of the pressure to not be different and participate in shameful behaviors in the sight of everyone.

We have the life of Philip, the apostle of Jesus as an example of acceptance and transformation. He was young when he took an interest in the preaching of John the Baptist and began to listen to him. He was cautious, curious, overly practical; a shy youth but with a sensible mind. He was named an "apostle" and as soon as Jesus told him "Follow me," he did, and immediately invited his friend Nathanael.

Of the four gospels, John mentions him the most and I would like to talk to you about Philip in this chapter. This so you can appreciate the acceptance he received when he met Jesus, his teacher, the way Jesus treated him, and how he was transformed. This can be your own experience today.

First of all, we can see that because of his sensible nature, Philip was not going to go after just any new religion or trend. He was a Jew, and it was Jesus Himself who sought him out and asked Phillip to follow Him. When Philip speaks to Nathanael about Jesus, he describes Him as "Jesus, son of Joseph, from Nazareth."

There are three very interesting encounters recorded in the Bible regarding the process by which Philip is confronted in different situations. These situations show us how his interactions with Jesus caused him to gain confidence to engage with Jesus by giving his opinion and asking him questions.

Before the multiplication of the loaves, it is Philip who is asked by Jesus as to where they could buy bread for five thousand people. Being so practical, the first thing he does is calculate how much money they would need to buy food for so many people, as read in John 6:5-7.

What I like about Philip is that he was a regular guy, from a regular family. The nickname he received from the other apostles was "curiosity," because of his insecurity. He wanted everything to be shown to him, he was timid at first and lacked imagination. But he had a fine soul and was very reliable, so much so that when the apostles were ready to serve the food he became the main butler, making sure they weren't lacking in any supplies. And he fulfilled his responsibility very well. In fact, his attention to detail and his meticulousness really stood out, he was systematic and precise. You can see that he made the choice to be excellent, outstanding, and as a result he set himself apart in everything he was asked to do.

The second time he is mentioned is when some Greek men ask him to see Jesus and he goes to speak to his closest associate. By this we see that he had no trouble recognizing authority or seeking the advice of others. Philip speaks about this with Andrew and together they go and talk to Jesus (John 12:21-23). I am surprised that in the gospels there is no mention of other apostles being part of this, but we can read about several instances when Philip shares with the Master, and Jesus seeks his advice or asks him questions. And I think it is for you to understand that even though you may be young like Philip, Jesus accepts you just as you are, with your own strengths and weaknesses. He will walk with you if you let Him, in order to achieve excellence in your life.

It wasn't hard for Philip to ask questions; he was very curious. And Jesus didn't mind being interrupted even when He was giving the most important sermon, because He accepted Phillip just as he was. Jesus valued his qualities and his heart. He'd rather Philip come to Him if something wasn't clear, as in the case when He speaks about the Father, and Philip says to Him: "'Lord, show us the Father and that will be enough for us.' Jesus answered: 'Don't you know me, Philip, even after I have been among you such a long time? Anyone who has seen me has seen the Father. How can you say, 'Show us the Father'" (John 14:8-9).

Neither is He ashamed of your immaturity and insecurities. Jesus wants you to approach Him with confidence and bring Him your questions. We can see, that little by little in his walk with Jesus, Philip's faith was strengthened. In the Book of Acts, we see him confidently preaching to everyone about Christ. "Philip went down to a city in Samaria and proclaimed the Messiah there" (Acts 8:5).

Philip became someone who was excellent and stood out in what he did; he continued to grow, and we see him speaking as a knowledgeable man in Samaria. Someone who had been mediocre and common became a distinguished person and his word was confirmed through signs: "When the crowds heard Philip and saw the signs he performed, they all paid close attention to what he said" (Acts 8:6). "But when they believed Philip as he proclaimed the good news of the kingdom of God and the name of Jesus Christ, they were baptized, both men and women" (verse 12).

Philip was a young man just like you, and by looking at his life you can dare to reach for greater things, because the Lord has put in you the skills that can be developed. Christ invited everyone to follow Him; His theme was "come and see." Phillip accepted this invitation, and in turn extended his own to others, inviting them to come alongside and find out for themselves.

Even parents can learn from Philip's example. Instead of sending their children to do certain things, they can come alongside and walk with them.

CHAPTER VI
DIFFERENT WORLDS

For many reasons, I believe this is a time of great progress in every sense. At the same time, events that have taken place in less than a century have also brought about a very definite cultural shift that has caused new generations to adapt very quickly to changes and innovations. As a result of globalization, the distribution of labor, and many women, who in earlier times stayed home and were the main influence on their children's lives, have now reached their own professional achievements and have gone out into the workforce. Due to this shift, family and social values have been shaken and changed in extraordinary ways.

In times past, the lives of parents were different in terms of music, dress, the way one carried himself with more decorum and care in romantic relationships. In contrast the youth of today prefer to live for the now, even when it goes against their family's values of waiting until there is a relationship based on true love. The Lord is the one who rewards you when you wait upon Him to fulfill His plans for you regarding sexuality and marriage.

The mother, who in earlier times was the one to engage the conversation and oversee all of her children's activities, has become physically absent, thus, children and teenagers are interacting through their cell phones, laptops and computers with people they know and people they don't know. For this reason, because they are alone, many become egocentric, introverted, and find it harder to express their feelings and share their problems.

Perhaps some of you have grown up with babysitters or with other family members, grandparents, siblings or other extended family members. Or maybe you grew up basically on your own without supervision, thus becoming exposed to the influence of people who were not always good. This is reality and we must not overlook it.

Even fashion and art have changed. Instead of expression through canvas or cloth, people began to tattoo their bodies, puncture it with piercings, painting graffiti on walls to illustrate their protests against institutions that are often no longer able to connect with them or help them with their angst.

In many cases, and as a result of divorce and unstable relationships, there has developed a dislike for the institution of marriage and commitment. The norm has become to live together, try it out to see how it goes and if it doesn't work out, they gladly return to their parents' house, to be single again as if nothing happened.

Because of this trend, the rate of teenage pregnancies has gone up. Consequently, single mothers now have to take care of a new life, and we see that in some cases, the fathers won't assume responsibility for that baby even though they were a part of that child's conception. There is great access to information through computers, and with that to pornography, a fact that further tarnishes the beauty of sex in its rightful place, i.e. as an act of love and lifelong devotion. This is why as a mentor, I want you to realize that as a child of The Light (child of God) you are different and as such, the life you live will have greater impact upon a society that continues in its moral decline.

In the area of work, the trend is divided between those young people who have access to a university education and those who enter the job market after high school choosing not to pursue formal career training.

Regarding entertainment, we see a generation that leans more towards being sedentary. Finding pleasure in staying indoors and spending hours in front of a computer, being engrossed in virtual battles where they don't have to move a single muscle. There is no expenditure of physical energy. Obesity and inactivity, with resulting health problems, have become much more noticeable among our youth.

I pause to ask you: do you consider yourself "chosen for the process of transformation"? Let me mention something about the Internet to highlight the breakneck speed of technological advancement of the masses; it is extraordinary. Just by a few clicks or searching: "n in math," you get exact definitions and find what you're looking for. In this case, I use the example of the n in math to see our theme and reason of your exponential stance of being excellent, outstanding and set apart.

Regarding great exponents, I ask you the question (from Google): Do you want to know what the number n represents? "…there is a series of numbers so extensive that it would take a very long time to complete them, quite a few are written, and they end in n: $1,3,5,7…n$." A bit more, "It is usual to say that something is raised to the nth power" when it has a very high value. For example, "wisdom raised to the nth power." (Google) free access to show you how much is coming to you, without going to extremes.

For this reason, when the concepts we are dealing with here begin to take root in your life, you will change as a result of your intimate relationship with Jesus. He will Help you become a different person in a generation that is susceptible to the things mentioned above.

In regards to educational standards, these have also changed. Generally speaking, young people don't engage with people of other ages, don't think it necessary to greet people or introduce themselves, they don't say please or thank you. There are always exceptions, but I see that it is not uncommon for youth to disregard adult or older people's ideas or experiences. There is no fostering of a space for healthy interactions, rather, young people look for their own groups, their urban tribe of like-minded people. We must examine our feelings, thoughts and actions in order to understand the difference between current trends and our own Christian values.

As we have been talking about being excellent, outstanding and set apart, I wanted to include this chapter so that, upon examination, you will be able to see what difficulties you are facing. As I mentioned earlier, the exchange of ideas and of experiences will always be necessary so that you can receive instruction that will train you in the moral sphere of your character, and in your acquired knowledge, that comes from individuals who received training before you did.

CHAPTER VII
TRUE FRIENDSHIPS

Do you spend a lot of time sharing your experiences with someone who thinks like you do? There is a phrase that relates to this: "Don't waste your time giving messages to those who DON'T respond, or words to those who don't listen."

The Book of Proverbs (18:24) speaks about reliable friends. "There is a friend who sticks closer than a brother." Jesus spent a lot of time with His disciples, ultimately becoming friends with them. Young people must receive Christ in order to understand the value of being in fellowship with the true and holy God, who said that if we obey Him, He will no longer call us servants, but friends.

In many biblical passages, God helps us understand the importance of choosing good friends. But young people who are only interested in the here and now, and not in forming lasting relationships, have a hard time grasping these principles.

Normally we give thought to a past experience, not one that is still in the future.

For them, the present is where they like to be. They need immediate fulfillment to feel loved, and to love and be accepted. From that point they choose according to their needs, not according to what is good for them. They operate on feelings and they let themselves be influenced by outward appearances or popularity.

When they reach a certain maturity and they are motivated towards excellence in everything, even in their relationships, they begin to be more selective and take the time to get to know people at a deeper level.

Proverbs 15:15-17 says: "A miserable heart means a miserable life; a cheerful heart fills the day with song. A

simple life in the Fear-of-GOD is better than rich life with a ton of headaches" MSG.

The period of academic formation from the time that you begin high school until you finish university, is precious in terms of the friendships you can develop. It is the right time to meet people from different cultural and family backgrounds without having the pressure of needing to please anyone in particular. Although it is true that you feel attracted to some of them, it is better to keep relationships at a friendship level so that you can get to know each other better, and try to avoid the exclusivity implicit in getting involved in a particular relationship with someone. Many true love scenarios emerge from friendship. And in any case, in order to know what you like you must first discover it. For that, you must first respect everyone and see how much they respect you.

The definition the Bible gives for love in 1 Corinthians 13:4-7 will give us an idea of the principles that apply to love, which is an essential part of all types of relationships: friendship, dating, marriage, as well as relationships with relatives, siblings, or parents.

"Love is patient, love is kind. It does not envy, it does not boast, it is not proud. It does not dishonor others, it is not self-seeking, it is not easily angered, it keeps no record of wrongs. Love does not delight in evil but rejoices with the truth. It always protects, always trusts, always hopes, always perseveres."

Where it says love, you can substitute the word friend and you will see the qualities required for true friendship. A friend that values the relationship will always be ready to defend you and honor you; your heart will be able to trust them because you know they will never intentionally try to hurt you. We need to develop the same qualities in order to grow in love, and nurture those same qualities from our childhood in order to enjoy good friendships.

What does it mean to choose to not only think about yourself, but include those who reach out to you, and above all, to having a friendly attitude at all times? It means being willing to receive in your heart, in your mind, and in your home, those who need someone to understand them, listen to them, and encourage them.

A good friendship must be based on honesty. It doesn't grow where there are lies, as these cause you to lose credibility in the face of your friend. Distrust kills the best of relationships. No one likes to feel deceived. Always and at all times, be truthful with yourself and with others. "Let us not love with words or speech but with actions and in truth" (1 John 3:18). Honesty matters.

Another characteristic is to not overly emphasize your friend's mistakes or faults. You should not be ruthless with other people's shortcomings. We all make mistakes, and the Bible says that, "Whoever would foster love covers over an offense, but whoever repeats the matter separates close friends" (Proverbs 17:9).

I also must caution you to the danger of choosing to make friends with people who have bad habits such as the type of conduct described earlier; people who don't have qualms about participating in illegal or immoral behavior. This reminds me of the passage in the Book of Jeremiah 24:1-10. The people of God had been taken into captivity to Babylon. Time after time, from the lips of different prophets, the Holy Spirit had admonished them and told them to depart from their evil ways and their worship of other gods, but everyone had become corrupted, and in the end they were conquered and taken into captivity. At that time God gave Jeremiah a vision where he saw two baskets of figs, in one the figs were in good condition; these represented those who had been taken into captivity but whom God protected despite their condition. God said that He would watch over them and not hurt them. He would make sure they were well treated and would bring them back. On the other hand, the other basket had figs who were in bad shape, rotting. These were King Zedekiah and all those who were with him, who had fled to Egypt and who had not accepted the Lord's discipline.

They would be gotten rid of just as you would with rotten figs.

You don't put good fruit in the same basket with fruit that is decomposing, because the bad fruit will ruin the good. In the same way, Paul in 1 Corinthians 15:33 cautions us: "Do not be misled: 'Bad company corrupts good character.'"

Consequently, although it is advisable that you give everyone an opportunity regardless of their social class or education, since good habits don't depend on that, you must be selective if you realize that someone is not healthy or is lacking integrity. Distance yourself from that person. But don't lose your spontaneity or close yourself to friendships. Remain open-minded.

CHAPTER VIII
A SUCCESSFUL DATING RELATIONSHIP

In order to contemplate a dating relationship, you must get to know the person you like, who they are, what they have to offer, and what they want to do in life.

Many mistakes could be avoided if young people would just for a moment set aside romantic love in order to consider the differences that exist, so that the relationship can be a lasting one and not one that ends badly. Choices are often made with only the heart and not the head. Regarding dating, a relationship that should culminate in marriage (which is the whole purpose of dating) you have to take time to find the right person for you. For this reason, we have to make sure that the relationship flows out of true friendship, allowing us to get to know one another without pressure.

A saying that I think is very true is: "don't marry anyone unless you have spent a summer and a winter with them."

This can be taken metaphorically, as well as literally. Getting to know the other person and developing a relationship takes time, it must be allowed to mature. It doesn't happen from one day to the next.

Today's teenagers are confronted with the principles of relativism that include drugs, alcohol, sex, and obscene language. They tell you sex is natural, and that you can experience it without a lasting relationship, that love is "free," that it is part of the emotion of love.

As part of today's culture, young people see casual sex as something natural and practicing it outside of marriage has become the norm. Nevertheless, many have held onto and continue to value their purity until marriage, which in the long run brings them much peace, joy, and fulfillment. But it is also true, for those who have given in to temptation and had sexual relations outside of marriage, that the grace of God is the greatest gift of hope. In both cases, it is precious to be able to surrender our sexuality to God. Are you valuing that abundant grace in your life?

Single people who desire to get married need to understand that part of the decision is to save themselves completely for the other person until they arrive at the altar.

"Fall in love with someone who loves you more than they desire you; desire doesn't last, but love remains."

Although our consumerist society distorts the true meaning of sex, and perverts it both on TV as well as in the proliferation of pornography in magazines and on the Internet, the Bible commands us to flee from immorality. Dear young reader, keep yourself pure, don't let yourself be fooled or taken advantage of by your naiveté. You must remember, relationships that last a lifetime cannot be developed quickly. If you want to build something true, with real goals, you must establish strong foundations. You ought to live in moral integrity and sexual purity. It is easy for someone who is influenced by what they see to make unwise mistakes. What contributes to a lasting union is commitment and prior agreement from both persons to not fall into temptation regarding the practice of romance.

The apostle Paul gives advice on this matter in 1 Thessalonians 4:38; 1 Corinthians 6:18; and 2 Corinthians 6:14-16.

Marriage is like a "very special gift." It is like a package that has been wrapped in tenderness. The "special gift," which is sex, must be saved until the day or night of the wedding. Abstaining from sexual relations prior to marriage is healthy, beneficial and holy. It bears repeating that those who are not careful in this area fall into error.

The courting stage, the time before solidifying a dating relationship, is charged with many emotions. Each one feeling the need to please the person they like by trying to dress a certain way to draw attention to themselves, or flirting, or trying to be friendly and engaging. There is a strong influence coming from advertising, fashion magazines, trends that favor provocative behaviors in all contexts and that encourage immorality and addiction. These are what the Bible calls "the desires of the flesh, the desires of the eyes, and the craving to get everything one wants."

Which is why, if you love God, you need to choose to surrender your body as an instrument in His service. Don't allow temptation to take you on the wrong path. In 1 Thessalonians 4:3-8, the Apostle Paul encourages you to abstain from sinful desires.

If you've already had the experience of forming a friendship that developed into a dating relationship, you will agree with me that there are certain steps that will cause the relationship to grow and become more and more reciprocal in affection and happiness. These relationships are coming from sharing common goals and a common purpose.

As I said before, a couple doesn't need to rush into commitment. The encounters shouldn't push them to commit; it is better to wait until you know one another better. Don't open the door, as much as possible, and fall into the temptation of having sex before marriage, since the consequences often may not be overcome.

At a societal level, although it is now seen as normal, it is considered worse for the woman to lose her virginity before marriage, although virginity and holiness in the eyes of God matter equally for both men and women. Also, we need to consider the subject of teen/young adult parenting. This in itself can affect the young person's plans in regards to their future. It causes them to have to abandon their careers as a result of having to care for their newborn child and creates loneliness and feelings of abandonment if the young man does not take up his role as parent.

The idea has become popular that one should not go into marriage without first finding out if the other is "good in bed." This pressure causes many young people to engage in romantic acts, that is, they want to "sleep together," an act that actually has no relationship whatsoever with true love. It may be that young people don't understand what God has in store for them in the future, precious plans for their sexuality and for their marriage. Avoid getting caught up in the things of the world that promote sensual filth and the distorted images that cause you to look down on your values. "Do not arouse or awaken love until it so desires" (Song of Songs 8:4b). You can be completely certain that: "if you seek the Kingdom of God faithfully, if you seek it above everything else, all other things will be given to you as well" (Matthew 6:25-33).

Love has the ability to share what it has, give of its best, and look out for the best interest of the other person. In contrast, what we see today is that each person is seeking their own best interest. For a relationship, any relationship, to be successful, you mus surrender and give yourself completely.

True love comes as a response to God's love, by loving Him with all your heart, mind, and strength.

These are qualities that a young person is not quite ready to take on, to be consistent in the relationship, to make it last, because he or she has to focus on what should be at that moment, their preparation and training for a career. The insecurities that sometimes arise from a relationship between young people will cause distractions and an inability to achieve excellence. For this reason it is advisable that the subject of dating be tackled, when possible, after one's studies have been completed. Even so, it is healthy to be accountable to other people, who can help us decide if the choice of life partner is correct and spiritually sound. I apply this principle of "accountability" and as I type this, my wife and I have been happily married for 41 years, becoming an inspiration to other couples.

Take your time getting to know the other person before you ask them to have a serious relationship. Look to see whether they treat you with respect and dignity. Observe how they conduct themselves at home, how they treat their parents and other family members. Don't think that if they are disrespectful with their own family they will treat you any differently. You do not have the ability to change anyone. Some young people make the mistake of thinking that they will be the savior of those they love, that they will cause them to change. But it just doesn't work that way.

Unfortunately, as I said, many young people consent to give themselves physically before getting married. This is not useful, and neither is it healthy. There are many who suffer rejection and betrayal both verbally as well as physically and can end up having severe emotional problems. This results in them having to figure out how to overcome the horrible situation where a relationship comes to an end or the regret from having a one-night stand. These young people end up emotionally connected to people that aren't good for them.

What should you do if you are stuck in an unhealthy relationship?

First, try with all your heart to undo and cut that emotional connection, mentally, psychologically and physically with that person.

Second, decide not to see or be near that person for at least six months.

Third, ask the Lord to cut every spiritual tie, and heal the lies and the wounds; ask Him to cleanse your emotions and to restore your ability to love.

Many young people are bound up, enduring outrage and scorn. In order to be completely delivered from that "snare," trust in God; He understands your fears. He forgives your mistakes, and as the Bible says, "by the blood of Christ your life will be clean, your person restored."

Everything will be covered by forgiveness, since you said yes to God. Invite Christ to be a part of your life and your hope will be restored.

As Romans 15:13 declares:

"May the God of hope fill you with all joy and peace as you trust in him, so that you may overflow with hope by the power of the Holy Spirit."

These words will help you:

Infatuation is instant desire; one set of glands calling to another.

True love, on the other hand, is friendship that takes root and grows, one day at a time.

Infatuation is marked by a feeling of insecurity. There are nagging doubts, unanswered questions about your beloved that you would just as soon not examine too closely. You are e True love is the quiet understanding and mature acceptance of your beloved's imperfection. It is real and it gives you strength and grows beyond you. But near or far, you know he or she is yours and you can wait with confidence.

Infatuation says: Get married already. Don't risk losing him or her.

True love counsels: Be patient. Don't get scared. He or she is yours. You can plan your future with confidence.

Infatuation lacks confidence. When one or the other is away, we wonder if they're cheating on us. Sometimes you check.

True love means trust, full trust. Your beloved feels that trust. Nothing threatens your relationship.

Infatuation might lead you to do things that we might later regret.

True love lifts us up. It makes you look up. It makes you think up. It makes you a better person than you were before. (Ann Landers, adapted by the author.)

Twelve Steps for a Lifetime

Dr. James C. Dobson, in his book Love for a Lifetime, quotes Drs. Joy and Morris, who list twelve steps that result in bonding, the emotional connectedness that links a man and a woman together for life and during their courtship.

Eye to body. A quick view can reveal gender: The shape, age, personality and status of the person. The importance people give to these criteria determines how much attraction there is or isn't between two people.

Eye to eye. This occurs when a man and a woman meet each other and exchange glances; but their most natural reaction is to look away, which generally means they either feel comfortable or insecure. If your eyes meet again, they might smile, which is a signal that they might like to get to know each other.

Voice to voice. Their first conversations are typical, and include questions such as these: "What is your name?" "Where do you work?" During this extended stage, they learn about each other's opinion, their hobbies, activities, habits, what they like and don't like. If they get along, they become friends.

Hand to hand. The first time the couple has physical contact, tends to be a situation that is not romantic, like when the man helps the woman walk down the stairs, or avoid an obstacle. Up until that time, either person is able to leave the relationship without rejecting the other one. However, if it continues, hand holding will become proof of the romantic connection between them.

Hand to shoulder. This affectionate hug is still free from commitment. It is the type of hug between good buddies, in which the man and the woman are side by side. They are more concerned with the world in front of them than about themselves. Contact between the hand and the shoulder reveals that this is more than just a good friend, but it does not yet reflect enduring love.

Hand to waist. Since this is something that people of the same gender wouldn't do, it is a clearly romantic gesture. They both are close enough to each other to share secrets or have a private conversation. However, while they walk side by side, with their hands around the other person's waist, they are still facing forward.

Face to face. This type of contact includes looking each other in the eye, hugging, and kissing. If none of the previous steps was skipped, the man and the woman will have developed a special way of deeply communicating with one another through this experience, using very few words, and so arriving at an important point in the relationship.

Hand to head. This is an extension of the previous step. They stroke each other's head affectionately while kissing or talking. Rarely do people touch someone's head unless a romantic relationship exists between them or they are part of the same family. It is an expression of emotional intimacy. Steps 9-12. The last four steps of the bonding process are clearly sexual and private. 9) Hand to body. 10) Mouth to breast. 11) Touching below the waist. 12) Intercourse.

It is obvious that these last four steps of physical contact must be reserved for the marriage relationship since they are progressively more sexual and very private in nature Dobson, James, Love for a Lifetime Multnomah Press, 1990).

CHAPTER IX
YOU CAN'T IMPROVISE THE MARRIAGE COVENANT

The couple gets married and enjoys the satisfaction of serving the Lord together and sharing their lives as one. Getting married for such reasons is truly worth it!

The man and the woman, edified by their mutual respect, will complement each other because, according to the Word of God, the purpose of the household is to walk together in the same direction.

Love is more than nice words; you must learn more about the spiritual, emotional, physical, intellectual, and moral state of the person you want to develop deep relationship with. Both will choose to go through with their marriage vows in front of a minister and will say to each other: "I take you to be my wife/husband, to live with you according to what God has ordained for holy matrimony."

And there, between the two of you, you will commit yourselves to one another through vows of unconditional love saying: "I promise to love, honor, comfort you, submit myself to you and care for you, in sickness and in health, in times of plenty and in times of want."

The couple makes this promise for their whole lives. "I promise to keep myself for you, while I live."

And after that, the indestructible seal. "With this ring I marry you, becoming one with you with my heart and my life."

But the high purpose of marriage cannot be fulfilled without the following fundamental behaviors:

Exclusivity:

A good relationship must be exclusive, that is, it should preclude intimacy from being shared with anyone else, as this would violate its purpose completely as well as the tender trust one places in the other. When a person loves their partner deeply and exclusively, there is no fear of infidelity or for the relationship to fall apart. Of course, God's will is for marriages to last and not for them to fall apart.

One of the most prominent founders through the ages of sociology and the principles of psychology, French philosopher Auguste Comte said: "Marriage cannot achieve its main objective, which is the reciprocal betterment of the spouses, if it is not exclusive and indissoluble."

Of course, for this to happen, it is certainly necessary to know that we are here in this world to carry out a unique purpose, which is to glorify God and serve our neighbors. Spouses will agree to live in love and faithfulness according to the vows and promises they made.

We have marriages that are weak and unstable, almost disposable, because of a lack of God's presence in the home, ignoring the rules He has ordained as well as the practices of the basic principles that must govern every marriage.

From the very early days of our marriage, my wife Ester and I have learned to fully surrender to one another.

This is a daily practice. When we are willing to surrender like this, we can achieve the fine balance of submitting to one another within the relationship.

CHAPTER X

TESTS TO CONFIRM YOUR VOCATION

As a privilege of every moment.

The essence of God is excellence, and He wants you. to better yourself through the circumstances that present. themselves in your life. He looks for you to take in His teachings. He wants to test your heart to see if you are faithful, and what is great is that He wants your faith to grow, as well as your confidence that He will always be there to help you. If there is one person who wants your advancement, it is God. He will often stay silent when you are in the midst of a trial, to see if you will continue to put Him first and seek His counsel. He wants to know if you fully trust Him.

Isn't this similar to what happens with our teachers in school? If they are having you take an exam, they remain silent, observing to see if you are focusing on answering the questions or if you are distracted or trying to copy someone else's answers.

That is how God is. He seeks after us and He is always near to teach us. He wants you to know Him in Spirit and experience his supernatural, excellent, and wonderful nature. If you persevere, your graduation day will be a day filled with joy, fulfillment, and of seeing that the natural gifts God has given you together with your efforts to be better, helped you reach your goal. God has helped you by gifting you with intelligence, and so have your parents and teachers by giving you their input. Do not forget to thank them!

Reaching for the very best should be your purpose!

In fact, God will cause you to experience the very best!

Paul, the apostle of the early Christian church wrote to his readers and suggested "a better way." He told them: "And yet I will show you the most excellent way" (1 Corinthians 12:31).

Paul was showing them the model we can all aspire to: The extraordinary.

God has put that potential in you. So then, focus on what is before you and the future you are dreaming for in your life.

What can you say about your academic discipline? In this matter there are many issues regarding a need for interdependence: Improve your reading time, study the material more thoroughly, read many pages, and be specialists in your area until you become outstanding.

But if instead you only have excuses such as: "I'm not interested, the subjects bore me, too many presentations, I'm sure I will not graduate", etc. Or perhaps you say: "My classmates exclude me from the task." I could ask you: Do you want to be identified as one who is considered outstanding? You must make the effort, not just wish for it. "It is easier said than done." Simply said, we cannot deal with this subject in a superficial manner.

Often, we do not value the time spent in training and studies, and don't see it as a privileged season. Although it is difficult having to study wide-ranging subjects like history, or sociology, not to mention complicated ones such as calculus or math in my case, but you at least have the opportunity to access a secondary or university education, a privilege that is not available to everyone.

Of course, knowledge isn't achieved "with your head on a pillow." It is necessary for you to be disciplined, to decide on a waking time, and the amount of time you will spend on your studies.

Do you appreciate it when others encourage you to perform at your best? Sometimes it can bother us when people insist that we do our best when what we are feeling is powerlessness because we are overwhelmed by the scope of our studies. Do not be discouraged! We can always choose to do our best! You will find the answer to your questions, apart from the alternatives imposed by your professors. If you fail at something, you can always try again until you are successful. You will become exceptional, set apart, and excellent.

You will truly excel, ensuring your graduation or however you may succeed.

How will you achieve it? By being diligent with your studies, taking notes during class, doing research at home, and finding the available resources wherever they may be.

This is what I always say: "We must look at our studies face to face, head-to-head, taking advantage of the opportunity.

You are on the path to success! A tremendous challenge we should all enjoy. Unfortunately, not everyone sees it this way. Some young people immerse themselves in indifference and apathy. They lose themselves in empty dreams. They are distracted and lack motivation for studying. As a result, they don't change or improve.

What Is Your Dream?

What can a teacher do? I encourage you to think about your own situation, about your own progress in your education, and about your dreams and desires for a future career.

My motivation in writing this book is to add my work to that of the teachers. To encourage all of them to teach the very best classes possible so that the students will be good listeners, open-minded, and attentive.

The goal is for you to attain success from the education you receive and develop the gifts you have so that when you face challenges in your career, your intellectual abilities will be put to the test. But some young people are only theoretical. They don't put into practice the teachings they are learning; they think they will lose their spontaneity if they get too serious and responsible. They want immediate fulfillment, they don't accept challenges or frustrations, and they don't want to make any sacrifices. People say that "knowledge is power."

In this case, knowledge is being informed through academic means. But it cannot be just training in theory without values.

Applied knowledge combined with values is power! You should ask yourself, will the preparation you are receiving cause you to become excellent, outstanding, and set apart in your career without being unrealistic? Above all, remember that success in life is not measured by what you achieve without effort or what doesn't cost you anything, but rather through the challenges that you overcome every time you choose to go further.

"If you want to avoid unwanted results, do not continue in your apathy, you will not achieve anything that way."

In my role as a motivator, I ask students to consider this perspective, which has to do with gaining awareness of the investments they are making into their future.

CONCLUSION

May the Lord help you grasp everything I've presented in this book! May the Holy Spirit motivate you to surrender your heart and your affections to Chris!

In the most wonderful book ever written, the Bible, you can find the best choices for your life; its teachings help prevent failure and suggest paths toward a life filled with success and happiness.

The Scriptures declare:

"Remember your Creator in the days of your youth" (Ecclesiastes 12:1a).

Answer your Creator like this:

"For you created my inmost being you knit me together in my mother's womb. I praise you because I am fearfully and wonderfully made; your works are wonderful; I know that full well" (Psalm 139:13-14).

I remember something shocking and unfortunate that took place in Caracas, Venezuela. It is the story of a child who grew up with role models from the street, and consequently, ended up in jail. Once there, it was his mother who visited him and was trying to gather enough money for him to be set. free. What was incredible was that one day on one of those visits from his mother, the boy said to her: "Mom, I need to tell you something. Come close to the railing." The mother, trusting, came close and placed her ear towards him, and she screamed desperately: "You never disciplined me, never listened to me, you never had time for me."

Surely that poor mother had taken care of dressing and feeding him...but was unable to instill in him values for living a harmonious life as well as guiding him spiritually.

Young man or young woman may God light your way so that you will not choose the wrong path, but rather may you be nurtured by good role models so that you will not end up like that boy.

Take a moment to reflect on the following passage:

I gave your life but cannot live it for you.

I can teach you things, but I cannot make you learn.

I can give you directions, but I cannot be there to lead you. I can allow you freedom, but I cannot account for it.

I can take you to church, but I cannot make you believe.

I can teach you right from wrong, but I cannot always decide for you.

I can buy you beautiful clothes, but I cannot make you beautiful inside.

I can offer you advice, but I cannot accept it for you.

—Author unknown

I congratulate you for having read this book to the end, written especially for you, and now that you have read it, you may want to share it with a friend.

They will thank you for it! It will help them in the same way that I hope it has helped you to clarify your thoughts and attitudes.

The Word of God is a lamp for your life, and all who are willing to follow the wise path of obedience come into a personal relationship with the Lord, their Savior. He who set aside His glory and surrendered His life for you to have a new one! He is your hope, because if you belong to Him, you know for whom and for what you live, and you will be able to enjoy the abundant life that He offers you.

"To him who loves us and has freed us from our sins by his blood and has made us to be a kingdom and priests to serve his God and Father—to him be glory and power for ever and ever! Amen."

Revelation 1:5-6

I invite you now to explore the infinite universe of God's love, so that you will accept the reality of His grace that forgives all your past and raises you up so that you can reach His sure promises for your future.

God does not change. He is excellent, outstanding, and set apart, and as His child, you are also.

In Christ we find salvation. Receive it. He will take the blinders off your eyes so that you will be able to live in love, devotion, and steadfastness. And if this is your decision, I congratulate you. You will be guided by the light of His presence.

ABOUT THE AUTHOR

John Korszyk, M.A., M.Div. Marriage Counseling: John is a man who is ready to serve. He writes the way he lives and lives the way he writes. He received his training for ministry in various seminaries for theological higher education.

His perspective goes beyond Christian denominational boundaries. He has served as pastor, missionary, evangelist, and counselor. He is a graduate of Fuller Theological Seminary in Pasadena, California, where he received a Master of Arts in Theology, as well as a Master of Divinity in Marriage Counseling and Pastoral Care. Professor Korszyk is founder and president of Voice of the Family Ministries, Inc. His message focuses on bringing hope, restoration, and encouragement to families. For more than 35 years he has traveled throughout Latin America, teaching and preaching the Gospel of Jesus Christ through motivational speeches in schools and universities.

John was born in Paraguay in the year 1952 and grew up in Argentina, but is now an American citizen. His ancestors are from Europe. His parents were born in Russia and emigrated to Paraguay before World War II.

He now lives in the United States; he is married to Ester Mabel, who is a singer. They have three children: David Ivan, Jonathan Eric, and Deborah Lynn.

For more information:

Telephone: (562) 556-0620
E-mail: voice4you@int7.com
www.vozdelafamilia.org

www.ingramcontent.com/pod-product-compliance
Lightning Source LLC
LaVergne TN
LVHW020428080526
838202LV00055B/5080